Alan Trussell-Cullen

Australia • Brazil • Japan • Korea • Mexico • Singapore • Spain • United Kingdom • United States

Animal Disguises

Fast Forward
Yellow Level 8

Text: Alan Trussell-Cullen
Editor: Johanna Rohan
Design: James Lowe
Series design: James Lowe
Production controller: Hanako Smith
Photo research: Michelle Cottrill
Audio recordings: Juliet Hill, Picture Start
Spoken by: Matthew King and Abbe Holmes
Reprint: Jennifer Foo

Acknowledgements
The author and publisher would like to acknowledge permission to reproduce material from the following sources:
Photographs by Auscape/ Doug Perrine, p. 7; Digital Vision, p. 15; Getty Images/ Imagebank, front cover, p. 1/ Stone, pp. 10 bottom, 11 bottom right; Photolibrary.com/ AA/ David Stephen Miller, p. 4 top/ Aldo Brando, p. 5 top/ Brian Kenney, pp. 10 top, 13/ Dani-Jeske, p. 5 bottom/ David Paynter, back cover, pp. 8-9/ James Gerholdt, pp. 3, 12 bottom/ Michael Fogden, p. 10 centre/ Mike Powles, p. 6 top/ Robin Smith, p. 12 top/ Roger Brown, p. 4 bottom/ Tom Ulrich, p. 11 top/ Cliff Philipiah, p. 6 bottom; Photos.com, p. 11 bottom left; Thinkstock, p. 14

ISBN 978 0 17 012522 2
ISBN 978 0 17 012513 0 (set)

Cengage Learning Australia
Level 7, 80 Dorcas Street
South Melbourne, Victoria Australia 3205
Phone: 1300 790 853

Cengage Learning New Zealand
Unit 4B Rosedale Office Park
331 Rosedale Road, Albany, North Shore NZ 0632
Phone: 0800 449 725

For learning solutions, visit **cengage.com.au**

Printed in Australia by Ligare Pty Ltd
7 8 9 10 11 12 13 21 20 19 18 17

THE UNIVERSITY OF MELBOURNE

Evaluated in independent research by staff from the Department of Language, Literacy and Arts Education at the University of Melbourne.

Alan Trussell-Cullen

Contents

Chapter 1

ANIMAL CAMOUFLAGE

Many animals use colour as a **disguise** to hide from an enemy. This is called **camouflage**.

This tawny frogmouth is hiding from the fox. The fox is its enemy. The tawny frogmouth is the same colour as the tree it is sitting on. It wants the fox to think it is part of the tree.

This sloth is also hiding from its enemy.
The eagle is its enemy.
The sloth is the same colour as the tree
it is holding on to.

Chapter 2

HUNTERS' DISGUISES

Some animals are **hunters**.
The tiger is a hunter.
It uses its colour to hide in the bushes.

Running Words 100

The carpet shark is also a hunter. It is the same colour as the sea bed. It uses its disguise to catch little fish that do not see it hiding in the sea bed.

The tiger and the carpet shark use colour as a disguise to help them catch their food.

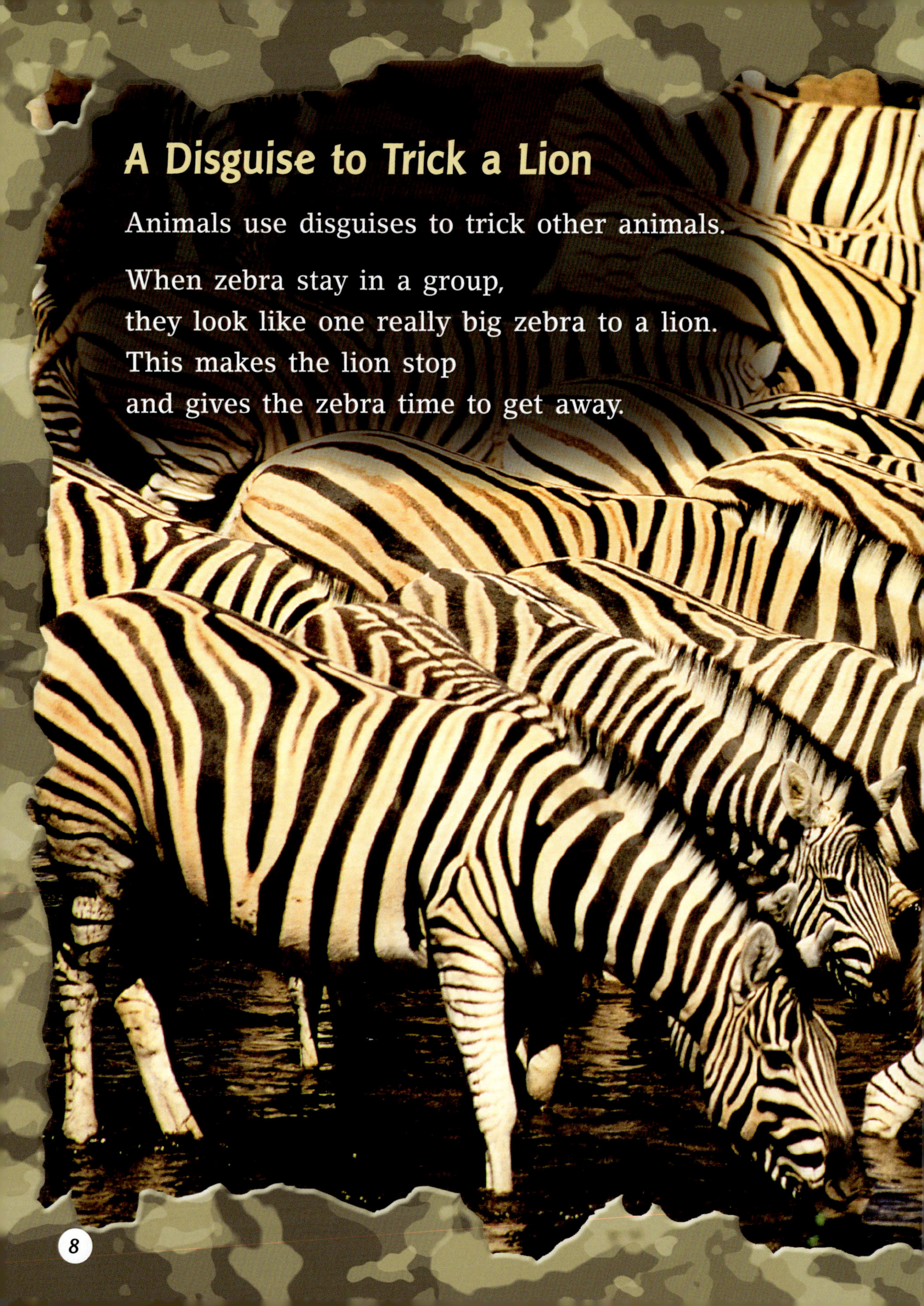

A Disguise to Trick a Lion

Animals use disguises to trick other animals.

When zebra stay in a group,
they look like one really big zebra to a lion.
This makes the lion stop
and gives the zebra time to get away.

Chapter 3

CHANGING DISGUISES

Some animals can change their disguise.
The chameleon can change its disguise.

It can change its colour from black to brown, yellow, green, blue or red.

More Clever Disguises

Some animals disguise themselves as something else to trick an enemy.

This stick insect looks like a stick.

This leaf-tailed gecko looks like a leaf.

The clearwing moth has a very clever disguise.
It looks just like a wasp.
This disguise helps to keep the birds away.
Birds do not like wasps, so they stay away
from the clearwing moth.

Chapter 4

PEOPLE DISGUISES

People also use disguises.
These soldiers are hiding from an enemy.
They have on the same colours
as the bushes around them.
This is called camouflage.